Drag

and

Sand-castles

Samuel Tate

To Nirmal wishing
you well and hope
you enjoy reading my
first childrens book.

Samuel Tate

ISBN:

ISBN-978-0-9957873-0-8

ACKNOWLEDGEMENTS

My whole-hearted thanks to everyone who has encouraged and supported me with my dream of writing these stories for children.

Above all, to Hilary, without whose knowledge and endeavours, this book would never have come to fruition.

Dedicated to my Grandson Cole,

who is my writing inspiration.

...do you believe in the powers of a child's imagination?

The **'Gramps and Me'** stories are page-turning adventures which are entertaining, full of suspense and contain many surprises… all of which will stimulate any child's imagination.

Each book is a 'must read' for any young reader and is perfect for adults to share with their young family-members as a bed-time story.

Book One

'Dragons and Sand-castles'

In 'Dragons and Sand-castles', Cole has been invited on a beach holiday in Cyprus with his Gran and Gramps.

While building a sand-castle, Cole suspects the beach rocks are beginning to move and his sand-castle seems to be getting bigger each day.

Can he be losing his mind?

Cole makes friends with two children, Appi and Ollie, but he begins to wonder if there is more to them than meets the eye...and then...

a pair of foot-prints in the garden ??

Contents

Chapter 1

A Sand Castle on the Beach

Gran and Gramps had rented a ground-floor holiday apartment close to a beach near Paphos, in Cyprus. I was invited to travel out on an aeroplane with them and stay in my own bedroom which they had prepared for my summer holiday. It was the first time I had travelled to Cyprus and the weather was really hot and sunny.

After a few days of taking me on a tour of the old town, we settled down to spend the rest of the holiday on the beach, which was just across a little sandy track from the apartment.

I collected everything I would need for the beach from my bedroom. Gran had brought toys and swimming trunks from home in her suitcase when we travelled.

With sunbeds in hand and a flask of coffee for Gramps, we headed down to the beach where we would stay for the rest of the day.

Very quickly Gran and Gramps had settled down and were resting on their sunbeds, reading story-books and drinking the coffee they had brought with them. I only drink water, so there was a large bottle beside Gran for whenever I became thirsty.

I was allowed to discover the beach by myself for a while to play on the sand and the rocks. Then I chose a spot near the sea and began building a massive sand-castle with a deep moat that went all the way around the castle, to collect all the sea-water when the tide would come in later.

There was still time to make mine the biggest and the best castle on the beach before I would be called to go home for our evening dinner.

I had found a flat piece of drift-wood and it was just the right size for the draw-bridge. I'd got lots of flags and toy soldiers, which would look great when I had everything finished.

It was a great beach and playing on the rocks was fantastic. In fact, the rocks seemed very spooky because one of them looked just like a dragon and another like a horse pulling a chariot behind it.

I was telling Gramps all about them and he said, "You have a great imagination Cole. I'll tell you what, if you like one night we can come down in the dark and see if they become real."

My Gramps is mad, he really is. How could they become real?... they are only rocks after all!!!

We went back home for dinner with the sea just reaching my castle and the water was quickly filling the castle moat. I ran away because I didn't want to see the castle being destroyed by the sea. I climbed on top of the rocks, pretending to be a mountaineer, before reaching the path that led us back home.

Chicken and pasta, yummy! It was great! I ate it all and asked for more and Gran said I was very good. We then had a pudding but I had the most! It was then a bath and a story, once I was in bed.

"Can we go to the beach and build another castle tomorrow?" I said when Gran cuddled me down into the bed sheets and I began drifting off to sleep.

"Of course, an even bigger castle if you want", she replied.

The next thing I remember was waking up with the sun shining through my bedroom window.

"Hurray! Ready for the beach everyone!!" I shouted, running into Gran's bedroom and jumping on top of Gramps who was still in bed.

"Come on, it's waiting for us."

"Slow down, it'll be there all day."

Gran smiled but Gramps just groaned in pain from my stabbing him with my wooden sword.

"Breakfast first and then we can take sandwiches for lunch, so we can stay there all day if you would like to. You will have time to build your castle and make some new friends. Maybe you can have a swim in the sea later," she added.

But Gramps didn't look up to swimming, especially when my sword almost removed his ear, making him disappear under the bed-clothes again.

I was so excited I ate my breakfast the fastest, and was first out of the door when everyone was ready to go.

It only took a few minutes for us to reach the beach and, as I climbed over and down from the rocks onto the sand, I noticed that my castle was still standing. Not only was it still standing, but it was bigger than I had left it yesterday!

There was water in the moat and a small boat sailing round the castle; it had a white sail and two small wooden pirates on it.

“Look at this! Can you believe it? Why hasn’t the sea smashed my castle? Instead, it has grown bigger and where did this boat come from?” I shouted.

“I don’t know Cole, but this little pirate look like a gruesome fellow!” Gramps said, placing the figure back on the boat and giving it a little push to help it on its way round the castle.

“Cole, I’ve never seen anything like this

in my life. It must be a miracle. Look… all the other castles on the beach have been destroyed by the sea and washed away, but look at yours! Wow!” he added.

Just then, I saw something move in the corner of my eye, in the rocks, something had moved.

Hang on… it wasn’t IN the rocks, it WAS the rocks!

I was sure the one that looked like a dragon moved its head and it just winked its eye at me. It’s not only Gramps that’s mad… I must be too…rocks can’t move! Can they?

Chapter 2

A lesson in Myth-olo-gy

I tried to act as normal as possible, digging Gramps in his ribs with my sword saying "Did you notice anything moving in the rocks?" pretending I hadn't.

He laughed and said, "Don't be silly Cole… rocks don't move."

"I know that Gramps!...but YOU did say we can come at night sometime to see if they become real and anyway, how did my castle get bigger then?"

"I don't know. We will have to ask 'the wise one'!" he said trying to calm me down.

"Who's the wise one?" I asked.

"Your Gran of course, she knows just about everything, or so she tells me. Let's ask her once she has settled on her sunbed."

I couldn't wait for that so I ran over and asked what was happening?

"Oh, it will be some of that Mythology thing going on," she said.

"What's Myth—olo--gy?" I stuttered.

"Let's all get settled and sit down and I'm sure Gramps will explain everything to you."

Gramps likes telling me stories and I could see by his face that he wanted to tell me something new. He puffed up his chest to speak but Gran spoke before he could get a word from his lips.

"Cole, you know that you believe in God and that He lives in Heaven?"

"Yes", I muttered expecting a Sunday school lesson.

"Well, thousands of years ago, many Gods lived on earth. Zeus, Apollo, Thor, and Aphrodite… these are just a few of the names I can remember.

In those times many strange things happened that couldn't be explained, even to this day. These rocks sound very strange to me. You carry on from there Gramps, you know more about this than I do, don't you?"

Gramps was great at stories because he made everything come alive and he even had a different voice for everyone in the story.

"Yes" he said, and began telling me a story…..

Thousands of years ago, Apollo walked out from the sea on to this Island of Cyprus for the very first time.

The weather was hot and the sun was beating down on his back, just like today. The sea was as blue as it could be behind him, so he stretched out for a rest on the golden sands.

He had swum for days to reach this land and, now he was here, he needed to rest awhile before continuing his journey and he drifted off to sleep.

He had come to Cyprus to meet a Goddess who he had heard many stories about and he wanted to see if she was as beautiful as he had heard. Her name was Aphrodite and she was the Goddess of Cyprus, the most beautiful of all the Goddesses ever.

Apollo was a good God, often called 'God of Music', but he was best known as the 'God and Protector of Health and Happiness.' This made him the most popular of all the Gods.

Gramps filled his cup with coffee before carrying on talking again.

Yes… he had fallen asleep on the sands. He was dreaming of the day he would meet Aphrodite and hoping they would become friends or maybe even fall in love, because when you are a God, you can't fall in love with just anyone, it had to be a very special someone....

"Just like your Gran," he whispered into my ear and continued.

When he was waking up, he was startled by something moving just below the surface of the sand. It was moving fast and directly towards him.

Apollo jumped to his feet and commanded whatever it was to stop immediately. To his surprise it did, but instead, shot upwards and out of the sand, and in front of him stood a giant of a man, more than three times his height.

He had large muscles that grew even bigger when he folded his arms in front of him.

"Aghhh, Aghhh" said the Giant in a booming voice.

"Go away and leave this island, you are

not wanted here."

Apollo was a little shaken by the sight of the giant and he stepped back so he could see the full size of him more clearly.

Then he spoke calmly to the giant, saying that he had come in peace and asked him,

"Please will you lead me to your Goddess Aphrodite, I would like to meet with her."

The giant stamped his foot, and the ground began to tremor, as he shouted

"No No! No! Go away or I will crush you into the sand!"

Apollo himself was not a person of violence, but had many powers at his command that the giant did not understand. So he asked again if the giant would show him the way to Aphrodite or, if not, he would in fact regret the aggression shown towards him.

"Aghhh! Go away little man!" said the giant.

Apollo waved his left hand in the direction of the rocks that rose gently from the sea and along the beach. They were dark brown and rugged, with lumps, bumps and holes that made them look very eerie and strange.

The rocks slowly began moving and a Dragon's head began forming. Suddenly, the rocks sprang into life, becoming a very scary looking Dragon, which towered above both of them.

The dragon lowered his face down alongside Apollo and glared fiercely at the giant, but spoke in a very gentle voice asking, "Master, what should I do with this giant?"

The giant was now very shocked by the

dragon's appearance and he tried to step backwards, but unknown to him, the dragon had curled his tail around behind him.

When he stepped back he fell over the dragon's tail. Moving swiftly, Apollo sprang up onto the chest of the giant and ran up to his face! With one foot on the giant's neck, he asked again if the giant would now lead him to meet Aphrodite.

The giant nodded his head saying, "You have earned my respect and I will gladly take you to meet with my Goddess."

Apollo waved his hand again and the dragon walked back along the beach, lay down and once again became rocks leading into the sea.

The giant asked if he could carry Apollo because they would move faster and, feeling no further threat from the giant, he agreed.

He sat on the giant's shoulder as they moved at great speed across the island. In just a short while they arrived at the village of Polis, where Aphrodite and her family were staying.

On arriving in the village, the giant offered Apollo his hand, which he gratefully accepted, before being lowered gently to the ground.

When Apollo stepped to the sand he was met by a guard-of-honour who saluted him for winning the friendship of the giant.

Apollo introduced himself to the guards who were surrounding the bath-houses, which Aphrodite was enjoying at that moment.

He asked the guards to take his best wishes and greetings to their Goddess, together with a message that he would like an audience with her when it was most convenient.

A guard raced away with the message and, to everyone's surprise, just seconds later, the beautiful Aphrodite stepped outside and met with Apollo.

They both fell in love from the moment they looked into each other's eyes and, although this was never recorded in the history of Mythology, they spent the rest of their days on earth, madly in love with each other.

"That is a real Myth from this island," Gramps added.

"WOW! Do you think we will see a giant on the beach?" I asked.

Just then, a rock behind Gran's head appeared to move and I shouted, "Look! See… it is moving!"

They both turned around quickly, and I'm sure they must have seen it, but Gran just said, "I think you two should come back one of the nights to see what happens in the dark."

"Can I bring my binoculars with me, and my compass?" I asked excitedly.

"Yes, of course you can, but I'm not sure if you will see much with them in the dark," Gramps said.

"Great! Can I carry on with my castle now?

Chapter 3

Two Children

While I was making my castle bigger, a boy and a girl about my age said "Hello!" and asked if they could play with me and my castle. I said, "Yes! My name is Cole." The girl said she was named Appi, and the boy was Ollie.

"What shall we do first? Shall we make it bigger with more turrets?" Ollie asked.

We all became involved in building the castle and soon it was more than twice the size than when I came to the beach that morning.

Ollie asked if I would like to have dinner with them and their parents, so I ran and asked Gran if it would be alright.

She said, "Yes, we know where they are staying along the beach. Don't be late back though, because Gramps wants to bring you back to the beach after dark tonight remember?"

"I've not forgotten Gran" I called, running fast to catch up with my new friends.

"Wait for me" I shouted.

Their mother and father were great fun and we played games while we waited for tea to be prepared.

While we were eating our meal, I told everyone the story that Gramps had told me about Apollo and Aphrodite and I was pleased that everyone loved the story.

I began telling them about the moving dragon rock and the horse and chariot on the beach near my sandcastle. But no one seemed interested and they all reacted very strangely about my ideas of the rocks.

The way Ollie looked at me made me feel as if I shouldn't tell anyone about the rocks moving, or that they looked like dragons and horses.

I was told it was time to go back to my apartment and the family said they would walk with me to say 'Hello!' to my grandparents.

While the grownups chatted, the three of us played a game of tag, chasing each other all over the beach. It was great fun and we were all out of breath when their parents called them to go home and get ready for bed.

"Great!" I said to myself. "I hope it's time for us to go back down the beach soon, it's beginning to get dark."

We went into our apartment.

"Put some warm clothes on Cole. It's getting colder now, and it will be even colder when you are on the beach."

Gramps was funny, because he was dressed all in black with a black Balaclava over his head, which covered all of his face except for two slits at the top, for his eyes and one for his mouth. He kept poking his tongue out at me saying, “Ugh! Ugh!” as if he was some sort of demon.

“Stop it Gramps. You’re scaring me! And how will I find you in the dark in all those black clothes?”

He passed me a Balaclava and said “Put that on and don’t bump into me on the beach!”

When we stood side-by-side, Gran said we looked like Tweedledum and Tweedledee!

“Come on boy! I’m getting excited! Have you got your binoculars and your compass?” Gramps said.

“Yes” I replied.

“Be careful you two, and don’t cause any trouble to anyone you might meet?” Gran stated as we left.

Chapter 4

Night Manoeuvres!

We walked slowly to the edge of the beach, letting our eyes get used to the dark. Gramps suddenly dived onto his stomach in the sand and began crawling along the beach towards the rocks.

I jumped on to his back saying, "Come on horsey!! Giddy up!!"

He let out a gasp! I had knocked the breath out of him. He managed to throw me from his back and roll over saying,

"Get off, you silly thing. We need to be very quiet or nothing will happen, so get on your stomach and start crawling."

I kept getting sand in my mouth (…it wasn't easy this crawling game, I tell you!)

Gramps was really good at it and looked like an army sniper without a gun, so I copied how he did it and soon was overtaking him as we arrived at the rocks.

"Right, let's rest here, and while I get my breath back, you use your binoculars to see what's going on… if anything," he whispered.

I took the binoculars out of the case, which I had kept in my jacket pocket, and said that I had my compass and whistle if we needed them.

I adjusted the glasses and started to look around the beach. The tide had been in while we ate our dinner and it was now going out again.

"I can see my castle and it's still good Gramps! There's a boy playing with the castle and he has long blonde hair. He seems to be talking to the rocks. The castle is massive!"

"Let me have a look," said Gramps, and

he took the binoculars from me.

"Blimey!..." he said. "You are right! If we crawl a little closer to the rock that looks like a chariot, we should be able to see and hear everything properly from there."

This was real commando action now, as we had to be really quiet and not be seen by the boy in case we frightened him away.

When we settled behind the chariot rock, Gramps said, "Well done, Cole! You will make a great commando when you grow up. Now, you keep your eyes wide open and watch that boy, while I take a rest to get my breath back!"

I could see the boy now and I didn't need the binoculars.

"He's talking to the rock that looks like a dragon and the dragon is nodding his head to the boy. The boy just said 'it won't be long now'... What won't be long

Gramps?" I asked, and a whisper came back.

"I don't know, but you must talk in whispers or we will be heard. Stay as quiet as you can." It was quiet for a while then he asked, "You're not frightened are you Cole?"

"No," I said, "but it's really spooky though!"

"Let's be quiet now. Let me rest… and Cole, keep your eyes wide open and let me know if anything else happens."

It seemed to be ages before anything else began to happen. Then figures in the dark appeared, three people… and they were walking towards the boy.

The smaller figure ran forward, and I noticed it was Appi! When she reached the boy she gave him a kiss and held his hand. The other two figures were their mother and father.

When they arrived, they greeted with a kiss and shaking of hands. They began talking between themselves, but quietly, and I couldn't make out what they were saying, so I leaned over to Gramps, to tell him what was happening.

"Did you see that?" I said, but when he didn't reply I pushed him and he fell over.

He was fast asleep! When I looked back again everyone had gone and the dragon was a rock again.

"Wake up Gramps! You've missed everything!" But he didn't want to wake up, so I had to pinch him and that made him jump up saying, "What's happening Cole?"

"Come on Gramps, it's time for your bed" I said. "No need to crawl."

He held my hand as we walked back home. It took me ages to get to sleep because I kept seeing that dragon's head smiling at everyone.

I decided not to tell Gramps everything that I had seen, because he might have thought I was making it up.

Chapter 5

A Cloak in the Castle

At breakfast Gran asked where we went last night.

"Secret manoeuvres, and only commandoes have privileged information!" Gramps said.

"We have nothing to report!" I added. She just looked at us the way she does sometimes.

"Let's go to the beach and see if the castle is still there and if it's any bigger!" I called.

It's real spooky now, but I wondered if it had something to do with that blonde boy who I saw last night.

Gran held my hand as we walked straight to the castle.

"Wow! she said. This is great Cole! You can lie down inside the walls… and it looks like someone has been sleeping in this part of it. Look, here's some white material. It's a beautiful cloak! Who could this belong to?"

It was just like the one the blonde boy was wearing last night, so I asked if she would keep it safe until someone came and asked if we had found it.

The two children came running down the beach shouting, "Look how big the castle is!" and we all started laughing and playing in the castle together.

A little later, I noticed that Appi had climbed on the rock that looked like a horse and she was talking to herself and smiling.

I said to Ollie, "Your sister's talking to herself on that horse!" He looked at me strangely and said, "How do you know it's a horse?"

I said, "Because it looks like one, but

only a… little like one. Have you seen my binoculars, compass, torch and whistle that I had bought from the shops by the harbour?"

Ollie thought they were great, so we played soldiers and commandoes until Gran shouted that lunch was ready and we all raced over to get some food, even Appi, but she seemed sad to come away from the rocks.

After lunch we were making sand castles. Ollie had gone to fetch some of his toys for us to play with. I asked Appi if the rock she had been playing on looked like a horse to her, and the one behind like a Roman Chariot. She asked, "Can you really see that in the rocks?" and I said "Yes…. and that one over there looks like a dragon, and I was sure I had seen its head move yesterday!"

Appi became very quiet, and carried on making sand castles, until she saw Ollie running towards us along the beach. She whispered to me.

“Can you sneak out of your house tonight around 11 o’clock and come here?” I said

“Yes…. I will be here.”

“Don’t tell anyone…. not even Ollie” she said, as she ran away straight passed him shouting “See ya later! And please bring the cloak with you!”

Then she was gone. How did she know I had the cloak? I wondered.

Ollie had brought some knights and soldiers and we played all afternoon, battling each other in the castle.

I was called to go in early for dinner, because we had agreed to go for a walk to the woods before dark. All the time we were walking I was trying to plan how I could sneak out of the apartment so late at night. I had never done anything like it before, even at home with my Mother.

By the time we returned from our walk I had decided that the only way to escape was to jump from my bedroom window, which was at the back of the apartment.

Chapter 6

A Secret Meeting

I was so excited, that I asked if I could go to bed early. Oops! That was a mistake. It made everyone look at me and I felt my face go red, so I said "Can I keep the cloak we found in the castle in my room tonight and can I have a story after my bath? I have big plans for my castle tomorrow. Isn't it amazing how it never gets broken by the sea when it comes in, isn't it?"

I always find that if I keep talking about anything for long enough Gran gives up trying to guess what I am up to.

It was half past eight by the time the story was finished, but I was frightened of going to sleep in case I slept right through till the morning.

"How do I keep awake?" I kept saying to myself, but then I was asleep.

The next thing I remember, it was very dark outside so I reached for the clock that was on top of the chest of drawers near the window.

“10.45! Wow! That was lucky” I said to myself, and began to get dressed. The window opened with a squeak, which made me very nervous in case Gran or Gramps heard it.

Had they gone to bed?... I wondered. Too late now though, I am going!

I found the cloak and tied it around my neck. It made me feel like I was Superman!

Then I opened the window fully and climbed on to the window ledge, and waited until my eyes became adjusted to the outside darkness before jumping the short distance into the garden. My feet sank into the sandy soil, just missing some flowers that had been planted just the day before. I didn't wait to see if anyone had seen me.

I ran as fast as I could towards the beach. I was hoping that she wasn't teasing me and that this wasn't just a joke being played on me.

When I got to the rocks there was no one there, but it was probably not 11 o'clock yet, so I hid behind the rock that me and Gramps had hidden behind, the first night, and hoped everything was fine.

I scanned all around with my binoculars, and then I saw a lady walking towards the rocks. She was dressed all in white and was very beautiful, with jewels in her hair.

There was no one else with her and she was looking as if searching into the darkness.

She began quietly calling "Cole! Cole! Are you here?"

It scared me. How did she know me?

How did she know I would be here on the beach? I stayed quiet and then she said "Cole! It's Appi. Are you here?"

How could she be the same girl? She was so tall and today she was the same size as me. I couldn't stay hidden forever, so I slowly walked out from the rock and said

"Appi! I'm here. How have you grown?"

"Shush" she said. "Come with me. There is someone I want you to meet."

We walked towards the sea and she said,

"Come and meet Drakon. He is my best friend!"

At that, the rocks began to move, and a dragon stood up above us and lowered his head right by the side of Appi and he smiled at me. He was very big, bigger than the elephants in the zoo!

Just then, a blonde man appeared, carrying a bow and arrows in a sheath, which hung across his shoulder.

"Cole, this is Apollo! You have heard of him from your Gramps? I can see you have brought his cloak with you as I asked."

"Yes," I said in shock.

Apollo came towards me and I passed him his cloak. He spoke softly to me.

"Cole, you are very privileged to be with us tonight, because no one is normally allowed to meet us. But because you could see Drakon and the horse and chariot, we know you are someone special, so we decided that we would like you to know our secret."

"Are you Aphrodite then?" I asked the lady. She nodded and smiled.

We sat on the beach and Apollo told me how they had met all those years ago, when the Gods lived on earth. They fell in love and eventually went to live together in Heaven.

"It's not written in the Mythology legends, so you must keep it a secret, or it would upset the whole of history if you don't. Can you keep it a secret Cole?" asked Aphrodite.

"Yes! Yes!" I said. "You can trust me!"

Apollo was speaking again.

"Drakon stays here, guarding our beach for when we wish to return to earth for a while. We like it here, and we can be children again. We have to leave now though."

He called out to the horse and it rose out from the rocks, followed quickly by the chariot. The horse was a beautiful snow white and the chariot golden and gleaming in the moonlight.

"Come, you can sit in the chariot for a

few moments before we leave, and thank you for letting me play with your castle, it was fun."

"So it was YOU who kept my castle safe then." I said.

"Yes, but tomorrow it will be gone, as will we," he replied.

"So, are you going to Heaven now then?" I asked.

"Yes, but the horse and chariot will come back tonight, and will wait with Drakon till the next time we call them.

Goodbye Cole," Aphrodite said, as she kissed my cheek. Apollo shook my hand and he lifted me from the chariot.

I stood watching, as the horse jumped into the air and they glided away, disappearing into the dark sky. Drakon said "Goodnight Cole!"

At 10 o'clock the next morning, both

Gran and Gramps were shaking my bed saying,

“Aren’t you getting up today?”

I jumped out of bed and ran down stairs and straight down to the beach. All the rocks were there all in the same place, but my castle had gone, no sign of it. It had been washed away by the sea. I ran over to where Ollie and Appi were staying, and even though I knocked and shouted, no one answered.

I ran back to the apartment saying,

“Where is everything? It’s all gone!”

Gramps said “Cole, have you seen these footprints in the garden just below your window?”

“I wonder who they belong to,” I said, and I also wondered how I’d returned back to my bed last night?

The End

Look out for

Robin Hood and ......

a Camper-van?

Gramps and Cole travel northwards to view a camper-van which Gramps would like to buy. Somehow they get more than they bargained for while test-driving the vehicle in Sherwood Forest.

Familiar names from the past appear from the Forest, leading them into a thrilling adventure against the Sheriff of Nottingham.

But will Cole and Gramps be up to this dangerous task...?

.... and many more stories in the

'Gramps and Me' series

About the Author

Keith Walker. Born in 1948, I grew up in the 'Black Country' town of Tipton, West Midlands, UK.
Having recently retired and realised I was finding more time to spend with my grandson Cole, which led us into many interesting adventures in the real world.

Through these adventures I began to write small stories of some of the events that took place. These stories became the starting point in writing the fictional stories of the 'Gramps and Me' series and, in order to portray a more 'child-friendly' character, I am using the 'pen name' of Samuel Tate.

Over the past few years I have been inspired by those 'special grandson' experiences which have led me on to create my 'Gramps and Me' series.

These stories have been written for those special moments when grand-parents/parents can share these adventures with their young family members in order to help children utilise their imaginations to the full.

I love letting my imagination run wild and find that writing stories is a fantastic way to do this. I hope my stories create opportunities which, I feel, are becoming less 'encouraged' in our new age of colourful illustrations, stunning visual effects, technology and everything else that comes with it.

My writing policy is all about allowing children to totally formulate their own scenes and scenarios as they read, or as they are listening to a story being read to them.

They may even feel inspired to draw their OWN illustrations of the stories, in which case I would feel my dream has been fulfilled!

samuels.parlour@gmail.com

17451335R00036

Printed in Poland
by Amazon Fulfillment
Poland Sp. z o.o., Wrocław